Happy Cat First Readers

First Friend

Kerry's family has moved house and she has a new school to get used to. It's a big school with lots of corridors and stairs so it isn't surprising when she gets lost on her way back from the library. But then a helpful dog appears and shows Kerry the way to the playground – and to all her new friends!

Happy Cat First Readers

First Friend

Christobel Mattingley

**Illustrated by
Craig Smith**

HAPPY CAT BOOKS

Published by
Happy Cat Books
An imprint of Catnip Publishing Ltd
14 Greville Street
London EC1N 8SB

Published by Penguin Books, Australia, 2000

This edition first published 2011
3 5 7 9 10 8 6 4 2

A CIP catalogue record for this book is available from the
British Library

ISBN   978-1-905117-39-0

Printed in India

www.catnippublishing.co.uk

For David, my first friend. *C.M.*

For Casey Russell. *C.S.*

1
New School

Kerry had been to school
for two terms. She had
made many friends. She
liked her teacher. And she
had learned to read.

Then Kerry's father
changed his job.

Kerry's family moved to
another town, and Kerry
had to go to a different
school.

It was a much bigger
school. It was three storeys
high. There were many
flights of stairs and long
passages with dozens of
doors.

In Kerry's first school there were twenty children in her year. In the new school there were one hundred about Kerry's age. There were four first

classes called by the points
of the compass: North,
South, East, West. Kerry
was in South.

Kerry's new teacher said,
'I am Miss Bell.' She was

short. Her hair was grey. Kerry's other teacher had been tall with golden hair almost to her waist.

Miss Bell said, 'This is

Kerry, everyone.'

The other children smiled
at her, but their faces were
strange to her.

Kerry had always shared

a table with friends. But
now she had one all to
herself. At her old school
the tables had been
arranged in groups. Here
they were arranged in two

horseshoes, one inside the other.

First of all they sang songs. Miss Bell played the music. There was a vase of cheerful daffodils on the shelf by the keyboard.

In Kerry's first school
there had been a bowl on
the cassette cupboard, and

the class had planted
daffodil bulbs in it. Kerry
wondered if they were
flowering yet.

Kerry did not know any
of the songs. At the end

Miss Bell said, 'Teach us
one of your songs, Kerry.'
But Kerry shook her
head.
'Tomorrow perhaps,'

smiled Miss Bell kindly.

Next they did maths.
Miss Bell gave Kerry a box
of counters, red, yellow,
green, all for herself.

'At my school we shared cubes,' Kerry said.

'We do it this way, by ourselves,' the children said.

Then Miss Bell said, 'You may go to the library now.'

2
A Long Way

The children hurried out
of the door, down the long
passage to the right.

They went across the
landing to the left, ran

down the stairs and across

another landing. They

passed an open door.

Kerry could see the

playground outside. But the

others went on down some

more stairs.

They jumped the two
bottom steps.

To the right and straight
ahead were two more doors
to the playground. But the

children ran round the
corner to the left.

To Kerry it seemed a very
long way.

There were some more
doors with the sound of

recorders coming from them. There was one door with a sound of computers.

The children disappeared through a quiet door.

Kerry followed.

3
Old Friends

A lady smiled at Kerry and
said, 'I am Mrs May, the
librarian. This is your first
day, isn't it?'

'My first day here,' said Kerry. 'But I've been to school before, of course.'

'Of course,' said Mrs May. 'Do you like reading?'

'Of course,' said Kerry.
'Then come here often to
read and change your
books. And you may borrow
books to take home

whenever you like. We keep
your bar code at this desk.'

'Thank you,' said Kerry.

She looked around the

room. It was much bigger

than the library at her old
school. All around the walls
there were shelves and
shelves of books. Many
more books than in her old
school library.

There were books about
trains and tortoises, horses
and helicopters, dinosaurs
and dolphins, mice and
mountains.

There were books on how
to make things. There were
books on how to do things.
Kerry thought that there
must be a book on every
subject under the sun.

Then on a low shelf
beside a big red rug Kerry
saw all her favourite books.
*Where the Wild Things
Are* and *Winnie the Pooh,
Peter Rabbit* and *Willy,*

Corduroy and *The Rainbow Fish, Babar* and *Each Peach Pear Plum* were all there.

The Very Hungry Caterpillar was there. And

so were *Madeline* and *Ping*.

Kerry was among friends
again. She gathered them
into her arms and sat down
on the red rug.

The only books she left on
the shelf were *Arthur*, *Spot*,
Hairy Maclary and *Harry
the Dirty Dog*. Kerry did
not like dogs.

The other children chose
their books. Mrs May
waved her wand over their
bar codes. They put their
books in their bags.

A bell rang, but Kerry did not hear it.

'Goodbye,' said Mrs May. 'It's time for you to go. Come back soon.'

The other children left.

But Kerry lay on the red rug with her friends.

No one knew she was there.

4
Which Way?

Mrs May came to put away
some books. She found
Kerry. 'Still here! It's time
you went.'

Kerry stood up slowly.

It was hard to leave her
friends.

'You may take one with
you,' Mrs May said.

It was hard to choose.

'What about *Arthur* or
Harry?' said Mrs May.

Kerry shook her head.
She did not like dogs.

'Do you know the way
back?'

Kerry nodded.

But outside the library
door she stopped.

The passage went left. It
went right. It stretched
long and empty, empty of
people but full of sound.

There were sounds of recorders from behind the doors where people played. There were sounds of computers behind the door

where people surfed.

At both ends there were
doors with glimpses of
grass and trees.

Kerry turned left.

In the distance she could
see stairs going up. She
walked to the stairs.

A big dog bounded down
the stairs.

Kerry stopped and stood
still. She did not like dogs.

5
Big Dog

The big dog jumped
the two bottom steps. It
bounded up to Kerry.

Kerry stood very still.
She could feel its hot

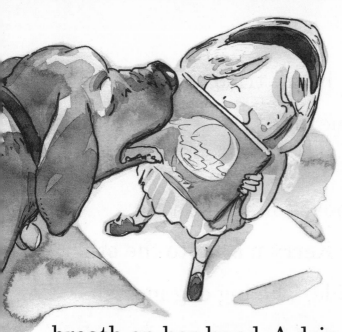

breath on her hand. A drip
from its mouth dropped on
her shiny black shoe.

She darted to the stairs.
The big dog jumped in her
way, in the middle of the
stairs.

Kerry tried to hurry to one side.

The big dog barked and moved in front of her.

Kerry moved to the other side. The big dog moved

too. It moved the same way.

Kerry turned around. She hurried back down the long passage.

The big dog followed.

Kerry came to another

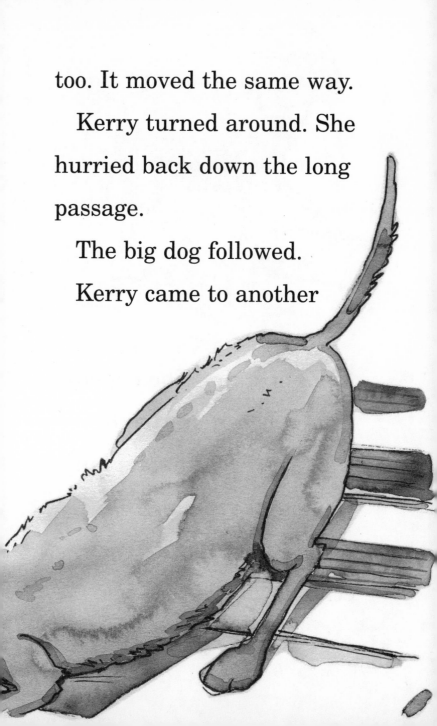

flight of stairs. The big dog
passed her. It started to
walk up the stairs, its tail
waving like a flag.

Kerry heard footsteps
echo down the passage.

She looked around. Mrs
May was walking away to
the other end.

Kerry turned back. She
ran as quickly as she could,
as quietly as she could,

after Mrs May.

She reached the bottom of the stairs.

Mrs May had gone. But the big dog was there again, on the second step.

Kerry said, 'Go away, dog.'
Her voice was swallowed by
the stair well.

The big dog barked.

Kerry turned and ran.

The big dog was at her
heels. As she reached the
other stairs the big dog
bounded past.

6
New Friend

Miss Bell was coming down the stairs.

'I thought you might be lost. It's such a big school, so many storeys and so

many stairs, such long
passages and so many
doors,' she said.

'But Big Dog has
found you.' She patted
the dog.

Kerry said, 'He barked at me. He stopped me going up the stairs.'

Miss Bell said, 'He knew they were not the right stairs. He knew you had lost your way.'

Kerry asked, 'Is he your dog?'

'Yes,' Miss Bell smiled.

'Of course he should not be
at school. But he is always
so lonely at home by
himself on the first day

after the holidays.' She

patted him again.

'He follows me to school.

He likes looking after

children on their first day.
He likes making new
friends.'

'He is my first friend
here,' Kerry said. She
patted his back very lightly,
very quickly.

Big Dog wagged his

tail.

'He is my first dog friend.'

'It is playtime now,' Miss

Bell said. 'Big Dog will take

you outside. He will show
you where the other
children are playing.'

Big Dog bounded up the
stairs. Kerry followed.

Together they went out of
the door to the playground.
Big Dog and Kerry ran
across the grass.

'Hello, Kerry! Hello, Big

Dog!' the children called.
'Come and play with us.'

They all joined in a game
together.

From Christobel Mattingley

The idea for this story came when
I worked in a school where the
library was in the basement.

One day a little new girl arrived.
At the end of her first library lesson
she didn't leave with the others.
After I sent her off to her classroom,
I wondered if she knew the way.
So I went to check and found her
on the stairs with a dog.

When I was her age I'd been scared
of dogs too, so I knew how she felt.
Now I love dogs and have many dog
friends.

From Craig Smith

I have always had cats. Once I had three cats and twelve kittens!

Dogs scared me a bit until I met my neighbour's dog. It's part Labrador, part something else. We're not sure. He visits me often, and sits outside my window while I draw.

The Princess and the Unicorn

Wendy Blaxland

No one believes in unicorns any more. Except Princess Lily, that is.
So when the king falls ill and the only thing that can cure him is
the magic of a unicorn, it's up to her to find one.
But can Lily find a magical unicorn in time?

Nobody is better at being bad than Buster Reed – he flicks
paint, says rude words to girls, sticks chewing gum under
the seats and wears the same socks for weeks at a time.
Naturally no one wants to know him. But Buster has a
secret – he would like a friend to play with.
How will he ever manage to find one?

Josie is Anna's best friend. Anna has played at Josie's house, she's even stayed for dinner, but she has never slept over. Until now...

The Magic Wand

Ursula Dubosarsky

Becky was cross with her little brother. 'If you don't leave me alone,' she said to him, 'I'll put a spell on you!' But she didn't mean to make him disappear!

Tom was given a gorilla suit for his birthday. He loved it and wore it everywhere. When mum and dad took him to the zoo he wouldn't wear his ordinary clothes. But isn't it asking for trouble to go to the zoo dressed as a gorilla?

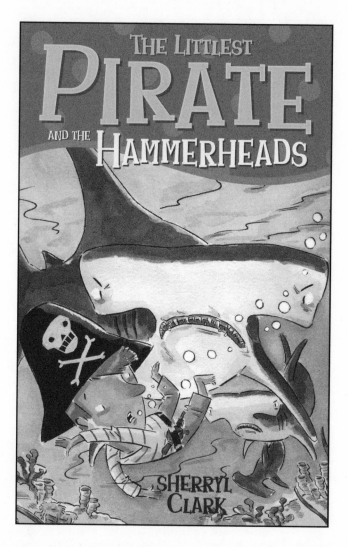

Nicholas Nosh, the littlest pirate in the world, has to rescue his family's treasure which has been stolen by Captain Hammerhead. But how can he outwit the sharks that are guarding Captain Hammerhead's ship?

David's had a party invitation!
It's a dressing-up party and he's going to go as a fox. But
when he arrives he can see he's made a mistake in choosing
his costume. Can he still fit in with the party theme and
have fun?

Jock can make a special sound like a duck!
If you can learn to make it too you can help Jock rescue the
little duck from the duck hunter. Quick, before it's too late!

Other Happy Cat books you might enjoy.

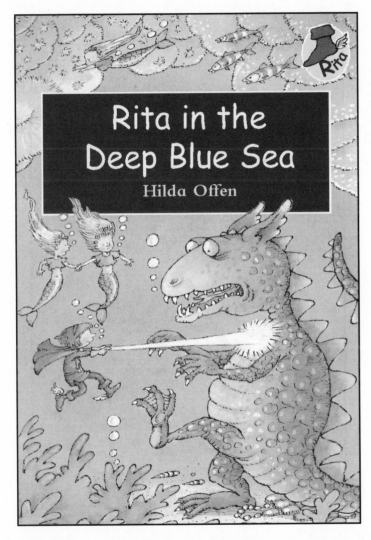

Rita's mother won't let her go on a boat with her brothers and sister. However, when she has changed into her Rescuer outfit she can ride on a turtle, tie an octopus in knots and even get the better of a mermaid-eating sea-monster!

Septimouse is the seventh son of a seventh son which makes him a truly magical mouse. Septimouse can talk to cats and humans too – he can even make them as tiny as he is. But the one thing he can't seem to do is to get his paws on some cheese!